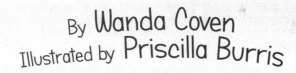

HEIDI HECKELBECK
Takes the Cake

By Wanda Coven
Illustrated by Priscilla Burris

LITTLE SIMON

New York London Toronto Sydney New Delhi

This book is a work of fiction. Any references to historical events, real people, or real places are used fictitiously. Other names, characters, places, and events are products of the author's imagination, and any resemblance to actual events or places or persons, living or dead, is entirely coincidental.

LITTLE SIMON
An imprint of Simon & Schuster Children's Publishing Division
1230 Avenue of the Americas, New York, New York 10020
First Little Simon hardcover edition January 2020
Copyright © 2020 by Simon & Schuster, Inc.
Also available in a Little Simon paperback edition.
All rights reserved, including the right of reproduction in whole or in part in any form.
LITTLE SIMON is a registered trademark of Simon & Schuster, Inc., and associated colophon is a trademark of Simon & Schuster, Inc.
For information about special discounts for bulk purchases, please contact Simon & Schuster Special Sales at 1-866-506-1949 or business@simonandschuster.com.
The Simon & Schuster Speakers Bureau can bring authors to your live event. For more information or to book an event contact the Simon & Schuster Speakers Bureau at 1-866-248-3049 or visit our website at www.simonspeakers.com.
Designed by Ciara Gay
Manufactured in the United States of America 0322 FFG
10 9 8 7 6 5 4 3 2
This book has been cataloged with the Library of Congress.
ISBN 978-1-5344-6114-7 (hc)
ISBN 978-1-5344-6113-0 (pbk)
ISBN 978-1-5344-6115-4 (eBook)

CONTENTS

Chapter 1

BUSY BEE

Heidi Heckelbeck was the *busiest* girl on the planet. Dad called her Lil' Miss Busy Bee.

On Monday, Heidi had swim practice with her team, the Little Mermaids. They worked on the butterfly stroke.

On Tuesday,
Heidi had Young
Rembrandts. It was
an after-school club
with her art teacher,
Mr. Doodlebee.
The club had been
working on a giant
aquarium collage.

Heidi made a pink neon jellyfish
from paper plates, paint, and yarn.

On Wednesday, Aunt Trudy took
Heidi to the Fine Arts Museum. They
got to see all kinds of original art,
from paintings to sculptures to videos.

Heidi's math tutor came over on Thursday—that's because Heidi needed help with word problems, especially the ones with fractions.

And, of course, Friday night was Movie Night at the Heckelbecks'. They watched Henry's favorite movie for the fifth time. Not that Heidi was counting.

Saturday morning was all about the swim meet. The Little Mermaids crushed the Aqua Maidens in freestyle and breaststroke.

Then, on Saturday afternoon, Heidi accidentally booked *two* playdates for the same day!

Luckily, Bryce Beltran and Laurel Lambert didn't mind, and they all played together.

And finally, on Sunday, Heidi helped her little brother create a costume for his history project. After that she had to finish her own homework.

Her whole family was impressed.

"How *do* you do it, Lil' Miss Busy Bee?" her father asked as he pretended to interview Heidi about her busy schedule.

Heidi pressed her hand against her chest. "Well, as you know, I have a FAB-U-LOUS social life, DAH-LING!" she said in a grand movie star voice. "And HOW do I do it, you ask?"

Heidi picked up her daily planner. It had unicorns and rainbows all over it. She pretended to show it to a wide audience.

"THIS is how I do it," she said. Then she hugged her planner close to her chest. "I would be nowhere without my trusty planner! It's the ONLY way I can keep it all straight, DAH-LING!"

Dad nodded thoughtfully. "And what if you ever lost it?" he asked.

Heidi placed the back of her hand against her forehead. "Oh, DAH-LING! I should simply be LOST without it!" she said. "Even a famous person such as myself needs to know when to study for math and when to go out on the town."

Dad laughed. "There you have it, ladies and gentlemen!" he said. "Lil' Miss Busy Bee keeps it all straight with a planner. And now it's time for a word from our sponsor."

That was Dad's way of ending the show.

PiNT-SiZE BEN FRANKLiN

"Where's my planner?" Heidi shouted on Monday morning before school. "I can't find it ANYWHERE!"

Dad turned from the stove and looked at Heidi. He held a spatula in his hand. He had been making pancakes for breakfast.

"Uh-oh! Sounds like Lil' Miss Busy Bee might be in a lil' bit of trouble," he said.

Heidi stomped her foot. "That is NOT funny, Dad!"

Mom hugged her coffee mug in

both hands. "Calm down, Heidi," she said. "Just take a moment to retrace your steps."

Heidi blew three quick, short breaths to calm herself. It didn't help at all.

"But I've already retraced my steps, AND I have looked EVERYWHERE!" she complained.

Then Heidi counted off the places she'd looked on her fingers. "My planner is not in my bedroom! It's not in my bathroom! It's not in my backpack! It's not in the kitchen! It's not even under the mail on the front hall table!"

14

That's when Benjamin Franklin walked into the kitchen. It wasn't the *real* Ben Franklin. It was her little brother, Henry, dressed like Ben Franklin. He was holding a kite and a notebook.

"I think you are looking for this," he said.

Heidi's eyes grew wide, and she shrieked so loud that Mom covered her ears. Heidi snatched the planner out of her brother's hand. Then she kissed the cover five times.

"Oh, my gosh, THANK YOU!" Heidi cried. "You literally saved my life!"

Henry raised one finger and used his best Ben Franklin voice. "It looks like electricity isn't the only thing I discovered."

Everyone laughed. Then Heidi inspected her planner inside and out. Everything looked okay, except for a few speckles of paint on the cover from when she had helped Henry paint his kite. *Phew!*

Heidi slipped her planner into her
backpack and sat down next to Henry
for breakfast.

"You know what?" she asked.

Henry raised his eyebrows. "What?"

"You actually look like the REAL
Ben Franklin—only pint-size," Heidi
said.

Henry smiled and held up his kite. The kite had a coat hanger for a string so it would stay in the air like it was flying. The end of the string had a key attached to it.

"Tell us all a little about Ben Franklin," Dad suggested.

Henry stood up and pointed to his wig. The wig was bald in the middle and had long hair on either side. "Hi, my name is Ben Franklin, and I am one of the Founding Fathers of our country," Henry began. "And I'm also losing my hair."

Heidi giggled.

Henry—or *Ben*—continued.

"And did you know my face is on the hundred-dollar bill? That's because I did a lot of really cool things, like when I was eleven years old, I invented swim fins. I also invented bifocals, which are a type of eyeglasses."

Henry put on a pair of fake eyeglasses and pointed to them.

"Another very cool thing I did was prove lightning is electricity when I flew this kite in a thunderstorm."

Henry held up his kite.

"From this experiment I also invented the lightning rod, which is still used on top of houses and buildings today."

Heidi raised her hand. "What's a lightning rod?"

Henry explained that a lightning rod attracts bolts of lightning and sends the electricity to the ground instead of hurting the buildings.

"I did lots of other cool stuff too!" Henry went on. "I started a magazine, and I helped write the Declaration of Independence. People say I also had a great sense of humor."

Then Henry bowed. The whole family clapped.

"Bravo!" said Mom and Dad.

Henry held out his arm toward Heidi. "I couldn't have become Ben Franklin without Heidi's help."

Heidi smiled. "No problem," she said. "Anything for my little Benny!"

Chapter 3

M.I.A.: MiSSiNG iN ACTiON

Heidi hopped on the school bus and walked down the aisle. She scanned the seats for one of her best friends, Bruce Bickerson. She didn't see him anywhere.

Hmm, maybe he didn't ride the bus today, Heidi thought.

Then she saw Bryce, her neighbor, who slapped the empty seat beside her. Heidi sat down.

"So guess what?" Bryce began. "Last night I made dinner for my whole family—ALL BY MYSELF! You wanna know what I made?"

Bryce was a talker. She didn't stop long enough for Heidi to answer.

"I made pizza skewers! And it was SO easy! All I had to do was thread pepperoni slices, mozzarella balls, little squares of pizza dough, and cherry tomatoes on sticks. Then my mom grilled them. After that we dipped the pizza tidbits in marinara sauce. It was SO yummy!"

Heidi smiled as Bryce roared on.

"And you know what my mom said? She said I should have my own cooking show. Isn't that SO cool?! Oh, and did I tell you about the salad I made to go with our pizza skewers?"

Bryce gabbed for the entire ride. Poor Heidi nodded like a bobblehead the whole way. She loved listening to her friend, but sometimes Bryce had A LOT to say.

When they arrived at school, Heidi hurried off the bus. She spotted Bruce getting out of his dad's car and waved like crazy.

Bruce didn't wave back, even though Heidi could tell he was looking right at her!

That is weird, Heidi thought.

Then somebody tugged on Heidi's backpack really hard! She whirled around and saw her other best friend, Lucy Lancaster.

Lucy folded her arms. "WHERE WERE YOU?"

Heidi stepped back in surprise. Lucy sounded really angry.

"What do you mean, where was I?" Heidi asked. "I just stepped off the bus. Was I supposed to meet you somewhere?"

Lucy tapped her foot. "I mean yesterday," she said impatiently. "Where were you YESTERDAY?"

Heidi tried to remember. "Well, I was at home," she began. "And then I cleaned my room, did my chores, and helped Henry with his costume for history. . . ."

Lucy continued to tap her foot.

"Why do you seem so upset?" Heidi asked.

Then Lucy threw her hands up in frustration. "Because YESTERDAY was Bruce's BIRTHDAY, and you were M.I.A.!" she scolded.

Heidi covered her mouth with her hand and blurted out, "Merg!"

It was the only thing she could say.

Chapter 4

BEST-FRIEND FEELINGS

Heidi sat at her desk and opened her planner. She had nothing down for Bruce's birthday. The only note on Sunday was *Help Henry with his history project.*

So Heidi flipped the page to the next week.

There, in big bold letters, she had written *Bruce's birthday*. It was in her planner, but on the *wrong* day.

Heidi sighed and looked over at Bruce, who sat next to her. But he was ignoring her.

Wow, Bruce won't even LOOK at me! Heidi thought. She could hardly blame him. Heidi would've been mad if Bruce had missed her party too.

Then Mrs. Welli rang a chime and called the class to order.

"Please pull out your writing notebooks," she directed. "Today we're going to write sentences using exclamations. Does anyone know what this kind of sentence is called?"

Nobody answered, so the teacher spoke up. "It's called an *ex-clam-a-tory* sentence."

Then Mrs. Welli explained that exclamatory sentences expressed feelings, like happiness, surprise, or anger. She wrote some examples on the board.

The class giggled.

"Now it's your turn," Mrs. Welli said. "I want you to write three exclamatory sentences."

Heidi tapped her pencil eraser on her desktop and tried to think of a sentence. She could hear Bruce scribbling something. Heidi peeked at his notebook. He had written: *I cannot believe you FORGOT my birthday!*

Heidi drew in a sharp breath.

Then Heidi wrote her own sentence: *I made a HUGE mistake!*

Bruce frowned and penciled a new response: *You really hurt my feelings!*

Then Heidi shot back: *I didn't mean to!*

But that didn't matter, because then Bruce wrote: *You made me MAD!*

And Heidi wrote:
I am SO sorry!

Then Mrs. Welli asked the students to share their sentences aloud. After a few students went, Mrs. Welli called on Bruce.

"Bruce, you've been quiet today. Would you share your exclamatory sentences with the class?" she asked.

Bruce reluctantly read all his sentences. The class giggled.

Mrs. Welli hushed the laughter. "Can anyone tell us what feelings Bruce is expressing?" she asked.

Natalie Newman, Lucy Lancaster, and Melanie Maplethorpe raised their hands.

"Shock!" Natalie said.

"Sadness," Lucy said.

"Oh! Anger!" Melanie added. "Like, anger at a bad friend, maybe. A bad friend who forgot Bruce's birthday."

45

Mrs. Welli clapped her hands. "Well done!"

Luckily, the bell rang before the teacher could call on Heidi to read her sentences to the class. As everyone packed up, Heidi tapped Bruce on the shoulder.

"Look!" she said, pointing to her planner. "I made a mistake and wrote your birthday down on the WRONG day. Silly me—right?"

Bruce shoved his notebook into his backpack. "It's not silly to ME," he said. "I have a birthday ONCE A YEAR, and this one was special. My parents rented out the WHOLE arcade."

Heidi looked at her feet. "I know."

Bruce clipped his backpack. "And then my best friend doesn't even SHOW UP," he went on. "Now you are making up an excuse about why you missed my party. I mean, do you even understand best-friend feelings?"

Heidi's planner dropped onto her desk with a thud.

"I'm really sorry," she said. "What can I do so you'll forgive me?"

"NOTHING," Bruce said as he ran out of the classroom. "Unless you can turn back time!"

Chapter 5

ROCK AROUND THE CLOCK

Hmm, Heidi thought. *Maybe there is a way to turn back time.*

She raced to her room the moment she got home. She pulled her *Book of Spell*s out and looked up time travel spells. One caught her eye. It was called Rock around the Clock.

Rock around the Clock

Have you ever wished you could fix a mistake in the past? Perhaps you broke something that belonged to somebody else. Or maybe you missed an important event—like your best friend's birthday—even though you really wanted to be there. If you want to go back in time and make things right, then this is the spell for YOU!

Ingredients:

1 watch
1 birthday candle
date of mistake
1 toy car

Mix the ingredients together
in a bowl. Then hold
your Witches of Westwick
medallion in one hand and
hold your other hand over
the mix. Chant the following
spell:

TURN BACK THE CLOCK
AND MAKE IT FAST!
I NEED TO FIX
A MISTAKE IN THE PAST!

"This spell should do the trick!" Heidi whispered, and she got right to work.

First she wrote down the day she made the mistake. Then she snagged a red toy car from Henry's messy room. In the kitchen she scored a birthday candle and a watch left in what her parents called "the everything drawer." It was almost like a magic drawer where her family kept the most random things.

Once she had the ingredients, Heidi zipped out of the kitchen. But before she got very far, Mom cleared her throat. Loudly.

"What do you think you're *doing*?" Mom asked.

Heidi froze. *Uh-oh,* she thought.

"I *know* those ingredients," Mom went on. "Toy car, birthday candle, watch . . . are you trying to turn back time?"

Heidi slowly turned around. *I am SO busted!* she thought.

Since it's always better to fess up, Heidi told Mom how she had missed Bruce's birthday party by mistake.

"I'm sorry, honey," Mom said. "And now you want to turn back time to fix it?"

Heidi nodded hopefully.

"Well, the answer is *no*," Mom said firmly.

Heidi frowned. "But WHY?"

"Time spells are very risky," Mom explained. "Even the best witches and wizards avoid them."

Heidi dropped the ingredients on the kitchen table. "So now what am I going to do?"

Mom picked up the toy car and rolled it back to Heidi. "You're going to think of *another* way to make things up to Bruce."

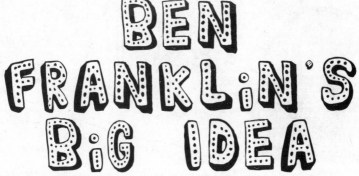

Chapter 6

BEN FRANKLIN'S BIG IDEA

Heidi sat on the edge of her bed and folded her arms.

"Oh MERG!" she growled. "If I can't use MAGIC to fix things with Bruce, then what CAN I do?"

Suddenly Heidi's door swung open. It was Henry—still in costume.

"Ben Franklin, at your service!" he declared.

Heidi shot her brother the stink eye. "Oh, go fly a kite!" she said.

Henry frowned and fake laughed. "Ha-ha. You are SO funny! But seriously, I heard you talking with Mom."

Heidi held her breath to not scream. Her little brother was a first-class super spy. Then she exhaled. "So what?"

63

Henry held up one finger and cleared his throat. He always did that when he had something important to say. "The honorable Ben Franklin once said, 'Do good to your friends to keep them.'"

Heidi rolled her eyes. "What is that supposed to mean?"

Henry leaned on her bed. "It MEANS you may have missed Bruce's birthday party, but what if you threw him a SECOND birthday party?"

Heidi's mouth fell open. She was ready to yell "GET OUT," but her brother was onto something.

65

"Oh wow! That is a GREAT BIG EXCELLENT idea, Ben Franklin!" said Heidi.

Then she hopped off the bed and hugged the pint-size bald guy.

"I better get started planning now!" she cried.

First she got permission from her parents, and they got permission from Bruce's parents. Then she called Lucy with the news.

"This will be the BEST win-my-best-friend-back birthday party EVER!" Heidi declared.

Chapter 7

TOP SECRET!

First Lucy came over to Heidi's house right away. Then Heidi and Lucy designed the party invitations on the family computer. They chose a border of balloons and confetti. After they found the perfect art, they filled in the party details. . . .

Shhhhhh!
Don't say a word!

We're having a surprise party for

Bruce Bickerson!

This Saturday
At 11:00 a.m.

Games! Bouncy house! Lunch!
And CAKE!

At Heidi Heckelbeck's
Party House

Heidi had her parents check the invitations—just to make sure there were no mistakes. Heidi was *done* making mistakes. Then the girls printed the invitations and sealed them in bright blue envelopes.

When they were done, Heidi slipped the invitations into the front pocket of her backpack so she wouldn't forget to take them to school. There was an invitation for everyone in their class.

"This party is going to be SO much fun!" Heidi said. "We're going to have juice from my dad's company. Aunt Trudy's making her yummy peppy pizza bagels, which Bruce loves.

And I'm going to bake him a special cake in the shape of a ROBOT!"

Lucy clapped her hands. "He's going to LOVE it, Heidi! I can't think of a better way to say you're sorry."

Heidi took a deep breath and said, "I just want things to be back to normal."

"Me too!" Lucy agreed. "Because it's no fun when friends fight!"

★ ⋆ ✳ ◎ ⋆

The next day at school Heidi and Lucy handed out the invitations to the entire class.

They had to be super sneaky so Bruce wouldn't find out. That wasn't too hard because Bruce was still avoiding Heidi.

"I'll come to the party!" said Natalie.

"Me too!" added Bryce.

Heidi looked over her shoulder.

"SHHH! Keep it DOWN, you guys!" she whispered. "Remember, the party is TOP SECRET. If Bruce finds out, it will spoil the fun!"

The girls promised to keep it quiet.

Then Melanie tapped Heidi on the shoulder.

"You can count ME in!" Melanie said. "And Stanley, too!"

Heidi faked a smile. "Oh yay! I was so worried that you wouldn't be able to make it."

What Heidi was actually worried about was Melanie saying or doing something to ruin the party. That would be THE WORST.

"I promise not to let Bruce know," Melanie said, and she pretended to zip her mouth closed. But Heidi was pretty sure that pretend zipper wouldn't work.

By the end of the day Heidi and Lucy had heard from everybody.

"Whoa, I think the WHOLE class is coming!" Lucy said.

Heidi frowned. "But how can we get BRUCE to come over?"

Lucy had a gleam in her eye. "Leave that to me. You focus on the cake!"

Then Heidi and Lucy grabbed each other by the arms and quietly jumped up and down. Their plan was working!

ROBO CAKE

On Friday night Heidi and her family crowded into the kitchen to help make a robot cake.

First Heidi shook a box of Devil's Food cake mix into a bowl. Then she added a box of chocolate pudding, sour cream, and vegetable oil.

Henry poured in the water and the eggs, which Mom had already cracked.

Heidi stirred the ingredients.

"Wow, this is just like mixing a SPELL!" she said, stopping to add the vanilla.

Mom laughed. "Only cooking is MUCH safer."

Dad plugged in an electric hand mixer and gave it to Heidi. "This will blend the batter better."

Heidi switched on the mixer.

Batter spattered everywhere.

"Oopsies!" she exclaimed.

Henry laughed and licked the chocolate specks off the counter.

Next Heidi scooped the batter into rectangular cake pans, which Mom put in the oven after setting the timer.

With the cakes in the oven, Heidi mixed the frosting. The kitchen smelled amazing!

When the cakes had baked and cooled down, Dad cut them into parts for the head, body, and base.

Then Heidi put the frosting on.

"Time to decorate!" Henry cried. He emptied a bag of chocolate candies into a bowl.

Heidi found two chocolate sandwich cookies, twisted them each apart, and placed the halves with the cream on the robot's head, cream sides up. "These are the robot's eyes!"

Henry stuck a tiny candy in each of the robot's eyes. "And here are its pupils!"

Finally, Heidi pulled out a lollipop and planted the stick in the side of the robot's head. "And THIS is the robot's antenna!"

Then they used white candies to give the robot a smiley face. After that they decorated the robot with rainbow candles.

Heidi stood back and admired their creation. It looked kind of sloppy. *Hopefully nobody will notice,* she thought. But Henry noticed right away.

"*Bleep! Bleep!* I am a ve-ry ug-ly ro-bot!" he said in a robotic voice.

Heidi sighed. "Oh you're right," she said. "My robot is a malfunction mess. Let's throw it away."

Mom put her arm around Heidi. "Oh, my little chef, remember, it's the thought that counts. Bruce is going to love it."

Chapter 9

MAD! SAD! GLAD!

Heidi peeked out the window on the day of the party. Then she announced to the crowd, "Bruce is going to be here any minute. Find a hiding place, and I'll keep a lookout!"

Lucy had invited Bruce on a bike ride to lure him over to Heidi's house.

Everyone looked for places to hide except Melanie. She was arranging the gifts on the coffee table. She placed her gift on top.

Heidi knelt down and stared through the front window. Soon the guests got tired of waiting. They came out of their hiding places. Of course, that's when Heidi squealed.

"I SEE them!" she cried. "Everyone, back in your hiding spots!"

The guests scrambled back into position as Heidi whispered a play-by-play.

"Okay, they've stopped in front of my house. Now Lucy's trying to get Bruce to come inside.  They are talking. And talking. Blah, blah, blah. And— *oh no!*—Bruce is shaking his head! I don't think he wants to come in!

Now he's getting BACK on his BIKE!
Lucy grabbed him by the arm! But
Bruce pulled away. Uh-oh! NOW
BRUCE IS LEAVING!"

Heidi jumped off the couch and ran out the front door. She raced down the path and cut Bruce off on the sidewalk.

"WAIT!" she cried breathlessly. She leaned on Bruce's handlebars.

Bruce wiggled the bars to get free.

"Please don't go!" Heidi begged.

"You and Lucy are my best friends in the world. And I'm so sorry for missing your birthday. It was the worst mistake of my life. I know you're mad at me, but will you please forgive me?"

Bruce looked up at Heidi. "I'm not
mad at you."

Heidi blinked. "You're NOT?"

Bruce shook his head. "To be honest,
I was mad at first. Then I was sad,"
he said. "I thought you missed my

party on purpose, and I was afraid if I talked to you, you might want to stop being my friend altogether."

Heidi smacked the palm of her hand against her head.

"Are you kidding?" she cried. "I could NEVER stop being your friend. We are friends for LIFE!"

A smile stretched over Bruce's face, and Heidi gave him a huge hug.

"Now I'm glad!" said Bruce. "But could you not hug so hard?"

Heidi eased up. "Only if you promise to come inside!"

"Okay, okay." Bruce chuckled. "Anything for a best friend."

Chapter 10

PARTY TIME!

"SURPRISE!" the guests shouted as Bruce walked in the door.

Bruce's jaw dropped, and his eyes opened wide. He turned around and looked at Heidi. "Is this for ME?"

Heidi beamed. "For YOU!" she said. "Happy birthday, round two!"

Bruce shook his head. "Wow," he said. "This is the best surprise EVER."

Heidi smiled wide and climbed on top of a footstool. "Okay, everybody, come with me!"

All of the guests followed Heidi into the backyard, where there was a bouncy house, balloons, juice boxes, and more! It was a birthday party wonderland!

"You got a me bouncy house?" Bruce cried.

Heidi nodded.

Bruce ran straight over, kicked off his shoes, and crawled inside. His classmates followed. They jumped, squealed, and double-bounced one another.

Then they played Pass the Parcel
and Musical Statues. Dad also
organized an egg-and-spoon race.
"Time for lunch!" Mom called.

Bruce sat at a large table in between Heidi and Lucy. Mom passed out pizza bagels while Dad served corn dogs and fruit salad.

Everyone talked, laughed, and munched. Then Heidi noticed something.

"Uh-oh. Where's Melanie?" she asked.

Melanie was nowhere to be found, and that probably meant she was up to no good.

"There she is," Bruce cried, "with a cake!"

Melanie was carrying Heidi's robot cake and singing "Happy Birthday." The guests joined in. When the song was done, she placed the cake in front of Bruce.

"Well, thank you, Melanie," said Heidi's mom. "I'll go get a knife and more plates for the cake."

As Heidi's parents went back to the kitchen, Melanie cleared her throat to get everyone's attention. "Nice cake, Heidi. Did a TWO-YEAR-OLD make it?" she asked in a snooty voice. "Because it sure looks like it was made by a BABY!"

Heidi felt her face heat up. *Oh no! I just KNEW Melanie would ruin my party!* She waited for the other kids to laugh at her cake. But they didn't. Instead, Bruce stood up.

"I think it's an awesome cake!" he said. "And even though it's little bit wonky and maybe a tiny bit droopy, and possibly a smidge melty—it's the cake my best friend made for me. And that makes it AWESOME!"

Then all the guests clapped and whistled—even Smell-a-nie.

"Well?" Lucy said. "What are we waiting for? Let's TRY it!"

Heidi's parents cut pieces of the cake for everyone.

Bruce got the first piece and took a great big bite of his slice.

"Wow!" he exclaimed. "This cake tastes BETTER than the one I had at my FIRST party!"

Heidi laughed. Then she picked up her party horn and blew on it. The coiled paper unrolled and squawked. Then *all* the guests began to blow their party horns.

Tooo-o-o-t!

Tooo-o-o-t!

Squa-a-a-a-wk!

Then Bruce put his arm around
Heidi. "You wanna know what? I'm
sure glad to have my bestie back!"

Heidi hung her arm on top of Bruce's. "Me too!" she said. Then they clinked forks and each took another bite of the yummiest ugly cake ever.

Check out the next book starring

HEiDi HECKELBECK

Heidi had a *hairy* problem.

No sooner had she tucked *one* side of her hair into her swim cap than several strands on the *other* side fell out. She stuffed them back in. Then a few more strands spilled over her eyes.

"Oh, merg!" she growled, and pushed those stray hairs back in too.

An excerpt from *Heidi Heckelbeck Pool Party!*

No matter how hard she tried, she couldn't make her hair stay inside that floppy old cap. "It's all stretched out," Heidi complained.

Mia Marshall, who was in line with Heidi, turned around.

"My cap's baggy too!" Mia said. She put her finger inside her cap, pulled, and let go. It didn't snap back like a *new* cap. It sagged.

Both girls laughed. Then Mia faced the pool. It was her turn to swim. She pulled on her goggles.

Snap! The strap broke.

"Oh no!" Mia exclaimed. "Now I

have to get another pair of goggles!" She ran to the locker room.

Heidi stepped to the edge of the pool and carefully pulled on her own goggles. Then she dove in. *Ahhhhhh,* she thought as she glided through the water. *I love to swim.*

After a few strokes, Heidi's vision became blurry and her eyes began to sting. *My goggles are leaking!* She stopped and shook the water from her goggles. Then she strapped them on and went back to swimming.